My Baba's Garden

Jordan Scott
Sydney Smith

WALKER BOOKS
AND SUBSIDIARIES

LONDON · BOSTON · SYDNEY · AUCKLAND

First published in the UK 2023 by Walker Books Ltd
87 Vauxhall Walk, London SE11 5HJ

Published by arrangement with Holiday House Publishing, Inc., New York

2 4 6 8 10 9 7 5 3 1

Text © 2023 Jordan Scott
Illustrations © 2023 Sydney Smith

British Library Cataloguing in Publication Data: a catalogue record for this book
is available from the British Library

ISBN 978-1-5295-1555-8

www.walker.co.uk

MY BABA

My Baba, my grandmother, was born in Poland, where she and her family suffered greatly during World War II. After the war she emigrated to Canada, where she settled in the small coastal town of Port Moody, British Columbia, with my Dziadek (grandfather). Together, they lived in a renovated chicken coop behind a sulphur mill, just off Barnet Highway. My Dziadek built railways and my Baba cleaned homes.

By the time I arrived in the world, my Dziadek had passed away. My Baba lived alone in the chicken coop and that's where we spent most of our time together. She didn't speak English very well, so much of the time we communicated through gesture, touch and laughter. We also communicated through our love of food. Even at a young age, I recognized that some of the ways she lived were different. She kept soap shavings under the sink until she had enough for a new bar. She stored food all around the house, in every nook and cranny. When I accidentally dropped food on the floor, my Baba swooped in to pick it up, kissed it and gave it back to me. She'd then watch me eat and say: "Eat! You too-skinny boy!" Sometimes she would laugh when she said this, other times she'd cry.

My Baba loved worms. Every morning, or after a rainstorm, she took me outside to look for them on footpaths and in gutters. Together, we put the worms into her lush garden. My Baba tried to explain why we did this by dipping her finger in rain and tracing the lines of my palm. She was telling me that when worms dig, they help increase water and air that gets into the soil and also provide nutrients. I am a grown man now and still pick up worms. My children do too.

My Baba would be proud.

– J.S.

My Baba lives in a chicken coop beside a motorway,

behind a sulphur mill

shaped like an Egyptian pyramid,

bright yellow like a sun that never goes to sleep.

My dad drives me there every morning.

It's still dark as we drive along the sea. I watch the sun
come up. The mountains look like whale bellies.

When my dad drops me off, my Baba doesn't come to the door, but I know where she is.

I let myself in and walk into the kitchen ...

and there she is,
hidden in the steam
of boiling potatoes,
dancing between the
sink, fridge and stove.

A hand holding a beetroot,
a leg opening a cupboard,
an elbow closing
the fridge door.

My Baba hums like
a night full of bugs
when she cooks.

Her house is crammed with food from her garden: jars of pickles in the bathroom, garlic hanging in the shower, beetroots on the shoe rack, tomatoes on the balcony, carrots in the rocking chair, apples at the end of the bed.

I sit at the kitchen table and wait to eat.

We don't talk very much. She points and I nod;
she squeezes my cheeks and I laugh.

My Baba makes me the same thing every morning before school: porridge, with lots of butter; pickles, cabbage and beetroot from her garden. I sometimes think I could swim in the bowl.

Every morning she watches me eat.

Sometimes I spill some. My Baba quickly picks it up.

She kisses the porridge, puts it back into my bowl and gently squeezes my cheeks.

My mum says that my Baba didn't have very much food for
a long, long time. I eat everything in the swimming-pool bowl,
and my Baba walks me to school.

When it rains, my Baba walks slowly. She hums and
sings songs I don't understand.

My Baba walks slowly because she is looking for worms.

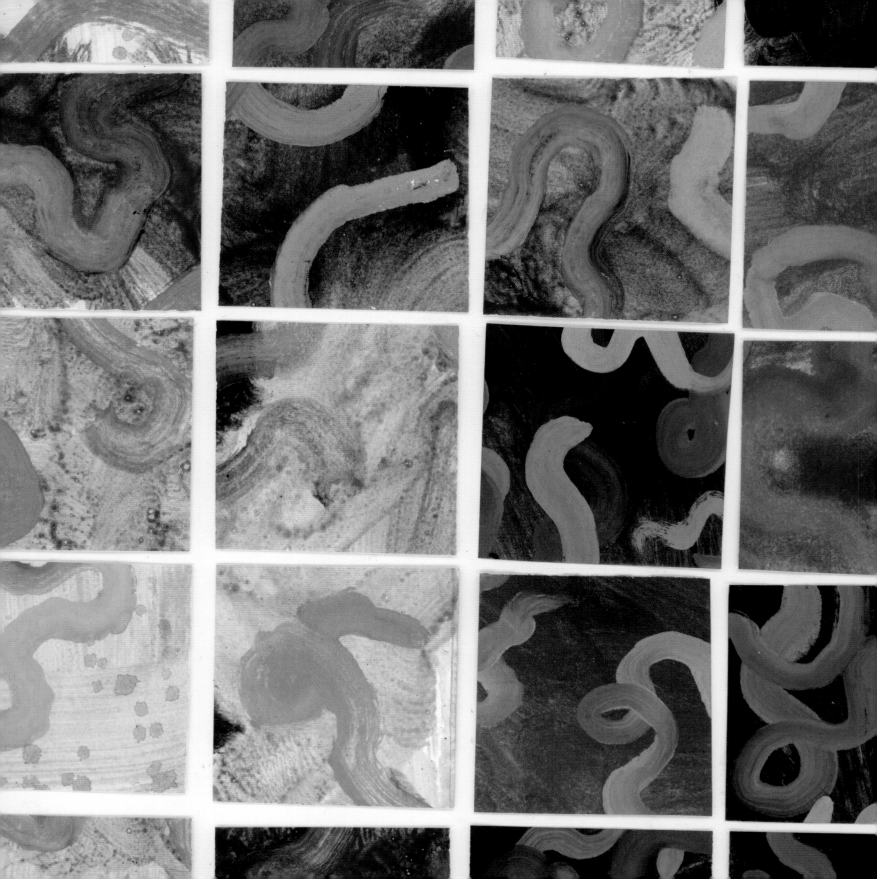

My Baba sees worms squirming in gutters and
puddles, worms in rain-rivers floating into the road,
wet worms with no earth beneath them. She picks
up all of them and puts them in a small glass jar
filled with mud that she keeps in her pocket.

After school, my Baba waits for me outside. We walk home down
the long footpath, along the sea, past the sulphur mill and into
my Baba's garden behind her chicken coop house.

There's so much to see, so much to smell, too much to eat.

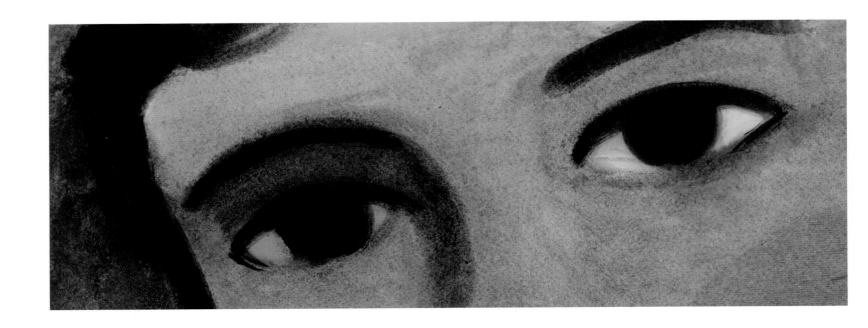

My Baba kneels next to the tomatoes, the cucumbers, the carrots, the apple tree. Her humming gets louder. She pours worms onto the soil and covers them with mud.

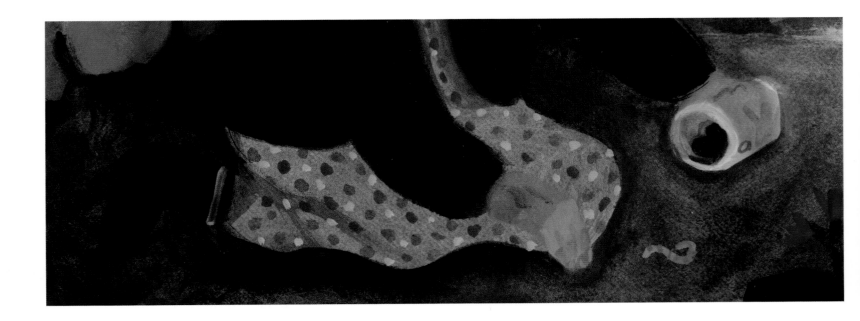

When I ask my Baba why she does this, she wets her finger
with rain and traces all the lines in the palm of my hand.

We kneel next to
the tomatoes,
the cucumbers,
the carrots,
the apple tree.

We pour the worms onto the soil and cover them with mud until the jar is empty.

This is what we do ...

until my Baba leaves her chicken coop home and moves in with us.

They put a big building where my Baba's house used to be.

Her garden is still there, but it looks like a jungle.

Now my dad drives me to school every day. I don't walk much any more.

My Baba sleeps in the room at the end of the hallway, right next to mine.

I bring her porridge and one sliced apple every morning.

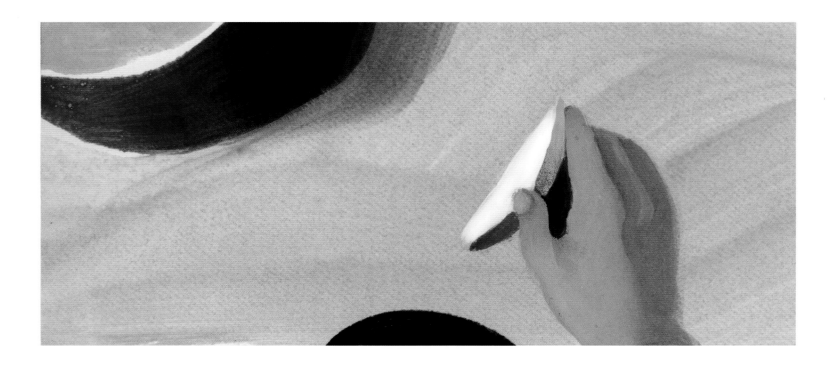

My mum and dad are too busy for a garden, but my Baba
kept seeds from her Sungold cherry tomatoes.

I planted them in a small pot that
I put outside her window.

I've never planted anything before.

I hope they grow.

My Baba tickles the lines in my palm with her finger. We look out of the window at the rain falling on the bright yellow sulphur mill and the mountains shaped like whales.

And I remember...

I run down the hallway and out into the rain.

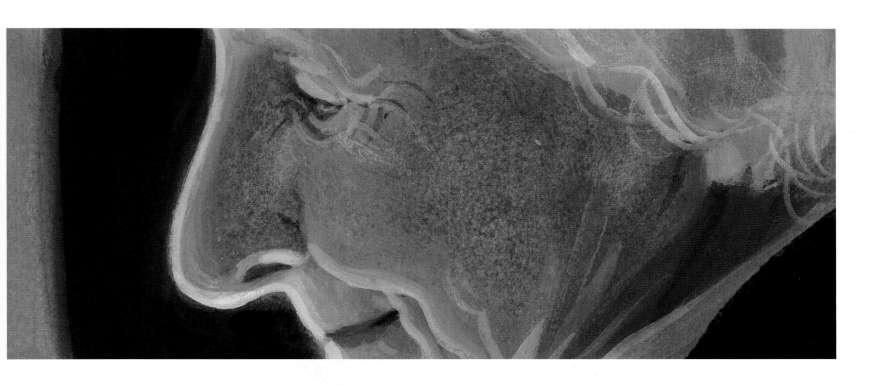

I walk slowly.

I pick up every worm I can.